D1126290

Messes
of
Dresses

Messes of Dresses

Dedicated to my husband who bears with all my hectic and frenzy deadlines. T.L.

First Edition - Sivan 5755 / June 1995
Second Impression - Nissan 5759 / March 1999
Third Impression - Elul 5762 / September 2002

Editor: Dina Rosenfeld
Layout: Gershon Eichorn

ISBN: 0-922613-75-3
LCCN: 94-80242

HACHAI PUBLISHING
Brooklyn, New York 11218
Tel: 718-633-0100 Fax: 718-633-0103
www.hachai.com info@hachai.com

Printed in China

Messes
of
Dresses

By F. Pertzig
Illustrated by Tova Leff

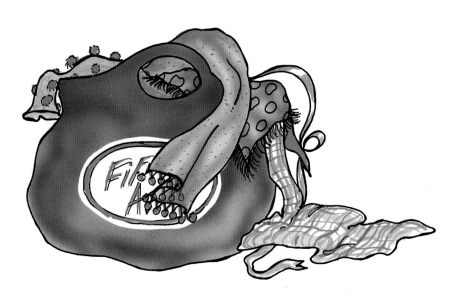

Hachai
PUBLISHING

איזהו עשיר השמח בחלקו

Who is rich?
One who is satisfied with what he has!

(Avot 4:1)

In a house on a corner
Inside a big tree
Lived sweet, sunny Gittel,
So happy was she–

That her friends all adored her;
No one could ignore her.
They loved to come over
For cookies and tea.

Her house was quite small; the rooms barely fit her,
The doorway–oh, my! It could hardly admit her.
Her kitchen was snug and her living room bare,
Except for a table and one little chair
Plus a raggedy sofa in need of repair–

And a pot of geraniums ready to bloom
And a yellow canary that sang a fine tune.
Of books, she had one–a small siddur, quite old
With a blue velvet cover and letters of gold.

On a hook on one wall was a green dress, all dotty
Which Gittel would wear when her blue one was spotty.
That's all that she needed. That's all that she had.
And she always felt happy, and never felt sad.

As she fed her canary and swept up the floor,
Gittel heard a loud "knock, knock, knock" at her door.
She smiled and she pulled the front door open wide
To welcome a guest who stepped right inside.

Knock!
Knock!

"I'm Sarah Saks," said the guest, "How are you? I've come all the way from Fifth Avenue!"

"Have some tea, if you please; I hope you can stay,"
Answered Gittel, who treated guests just the right way.

Sarah sat on the sofa and took a long look
And said, "Gittel, you've only one dress on that hook!"
"Yes, I know," answered Gittel. "No need to keep staring–
I keep that dress clean, and the other I'm wearing!"

"Two dresses—that's it?" was all Sarah could splurt.
"What happens if both of them fall in the dirt?
Or a plate full of noodles with ketchup and cheese
Falls from a shelf and makes stains upon these?

"Or what if you sit down on glitter and glue,
And a black magic marker and shoe polish, too?
Then what would you wear, Gittel, what would you do?
A green dress and blue dress are simply too few!"

Answered Gittel, "Two dresses
Are just fine for me.
I'm satisfied with what I have,
Don't you see?"

There was no stopping Sarah,
She fished in her bag,
And pulled out five dresses—
Each one with a tag.
Five dresses so fancy
That Gittel's jaw dropped,
Five dresses so stunning
That Gittel's eyes popped.

"This dress made by Lucci is silvery silk,
This one made by Shpent is the color of milk.
This pink tweedy suit came from Thallery's store–
Don't tell me that you've never been there before!
This shiny gold gown made by Dana Collide,
Has lovely lace lilies that go down the side.
And the grandest of all from Ganook de Laurent
Is bespangled with beads–it's all money well spent."

"I don't know," began Gittel. "My dresses are plain.
With fine clothing like this, I can't walk in the rain."

"That's silly!" cried Sarah. "No problem at all.
Just put on a new dress and let that one fall!
There's more where these came from–
All brilliant and new!"
Exclaimed Sarah Saks
From Fifth Avenue.

After that day, Gittel started to change
She had dresses to try on and hooks to arrange.
Five new hooks for five dresses appeared on her wall,
Then more and still more, till they filled the front hall.

Hooks, hooks, hooks, hooks were all over the house
On the walls of the bedroom she hung every blouse.
On the walls of the living room lengthwise and down,
Gittel busied herself hanging every new gown.
No room to serve cookies and tea anymore–
There were hooks in the kitchen and on the front door.

And this is how Gittel lived week after week–
So busy with hooks, she had no time to speak.

She thought about dresses all night and all day
She had no time for friends, and no room to play.

She talked about dresses until they said, "Quit it!"
Now Gittel seemed different, they had to admit it.

And soon they stopped coming to pay her a call.
And sweet, sunny Gittel had no friends at all.

Still Sarah Saks came, every day to her door
With dresses and dresses and dresses galore!
"Isn't it fun, Gittel, don't you look great?
With so many clothes, you can always rotate.
There's no need to wash, and there's no need to wait–
From now on, my dear, you will never be late!"

"Late for what?" burst out Gittel. She stared at the wall.
"And where would I go? I have no friends at all.
I can't move in this house; it is no longer cheerful
These messes of dresses are making me tearful!
Oh, how did this silliness all come to be?
Well, now I will fix it; just watch and you'll see!"

So Gittel began. She took down every dress
And unhooked every hook, till she cleaned up the mess!
She looked at Miss Saks and knew just what to say:
"You must take all these things someplace quite far away.
And please, you must do it right now. Yes, today!

I've learned something special, and here's what I know:
Aizehu ashir, hasameach b'chelko*
To be rich and happy, you don't need a lot;
You just need to enjoy what you've already got!"

* Who is rich? He who is satisfied with what he has. (Avot 4:1)

27

So Sarah Saks piled all the clothes up so high
On the back of a truck–and then waved good-bye.
Away went the dresses of silver and blue
The blouses, the suits and the fancy gowns, too.

Gittel entered her neat little house in the tree
With a smile on her face and a heart full of glee.
She picked up her siddur and said every word;
She watered her flowers and fed her small bird.
She baked sugar cookies and made some fresh tea–
And she said, "How I love being just plain old me!"